Rudey's **WINDY** Christmas

Helen Baugh & Ben Mantle

HarperCollins *Children's Books*

One Christmas Eve at Santa's house
amid the ice and snow,
the Clauses shared a festive feast
before he had to go.

Mrs Claus (who loved her sprouts)
ate each and every one,
but Santa fed his to a friend
until the last was gone.

"Bye bye, dear!" said Santa,
lifting one more sack of toys.
"It's time for me to go and visit
all the girls and boys."

Then Santa and his reindeer friends flew up into the sky,
the sleigh secure behind them and the presents piled high.

They'd just got to Australia
when Dasher took a sniff.
What **was** that funny smell
that had a sprouty sort of whiff?

"Oh, pardon me!" said Rudey. "But I think I've done a **pump**.
My tummy did a rumble,
then my bottom did a
trump."

The other reindeer giggled then they flew into the sky,
the sleigh secure behind them and the presents piled high.

The air was sweet for many miles,
then Dancer took a sniff.
Somewhere over China he had
smelt that sprouty whiff!

"Oh, dearie me!" said Rudey. "Now I've done a **windy pop**.
This is a bit embarrassing. I'll do my best to stop!"

The reindeer giggled more and then they flew into the sky,
the sleigh secure behind them and the presents piled high.

For a while the air was sweet, then Prancer took a sniff.
This time it was in India he'd smelt that sprouty whiff!

"I'm sorry, boys!" said Rudey. "But I've done a botty burp.
Why did I eat so many sprouts? I really feel a twerp."

The reindeer chuckled hard
and then they flew into the sky,
the sleigh secure behind them
and the presents piled high.

The air was sweet for quite some time, then Vixen took a sniff.
Just as they reached South Africa he'd smelt that **sprouty whiff!**

"Oh, excuse me!" said Rudey.
"What a smelly, stinky fluff!
I really wish this wind would go,
I think I've parped enough."

The reindeer laughed and laughed and then they flew into the sky,
the sleigh secure behind them and the presents piled high.

For a spell the air was sweet, then Comet took a sniff.
On landing in the UK he had
smelt that **sprouty whiff!**

"Oh, goodness me!" said Rudey.
"Now I've done a **great big toot**!
That really was a ripper from my
poor old **bottom flute**!"

The reindeer had hysterics
then they flew into the sky,
the sleigh secure behind them
and the presents piled high.

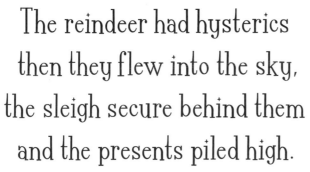

The air was sweet for hours and hours,
then Cupid took a sniff.
'Cause once more (in the USA)
he'd smelt that sprouty whiff!

"Forgive me, please!" said Rudey.
"But I've blown my **rear end trumpet!**
I can't believe there was enough wind
left inside to **pump** it!"

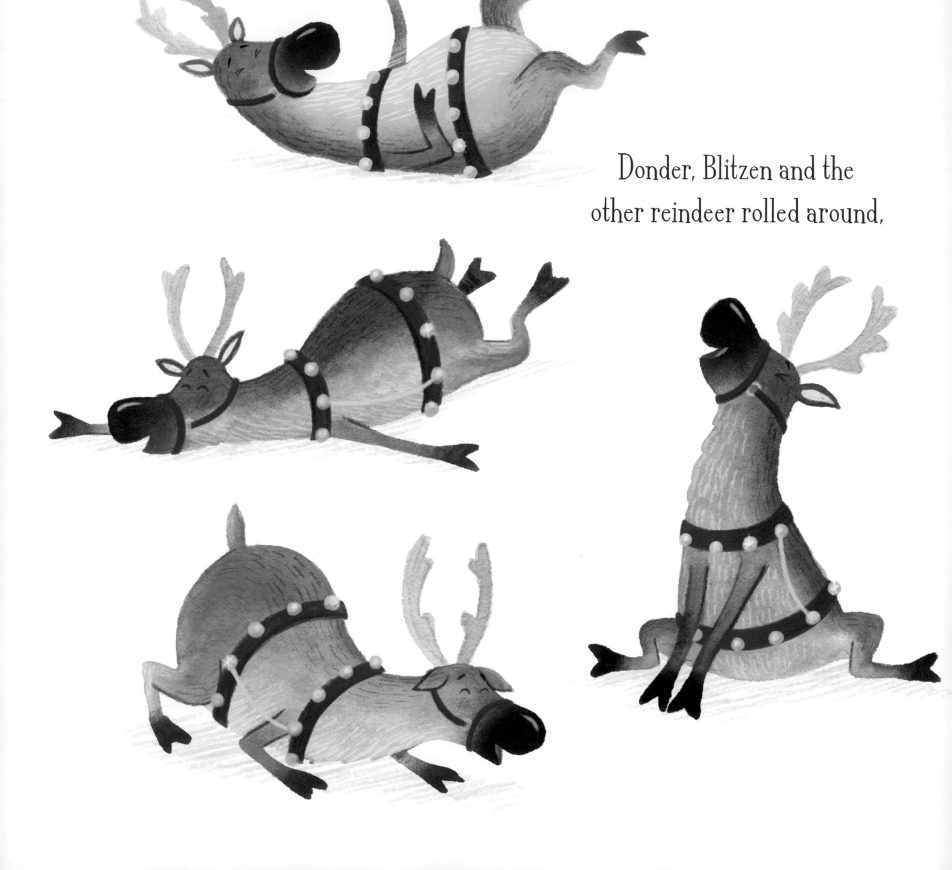

Donder, Blitzen and the
other reindeer rolled around,

doubled up with laughter
as they lay upon the ground.

"They've laughed so much they're out of puff!" said Santa. "They can't fly!
How ever will we get this heavy sleigh
home through the sky?"

"Some super-turbo gas
is what we need now!"
Rudey boomed...

He stuck his windy bottom in the air...

and off they **ZOOMED!**

But when they reached the North Pole
Santa got a **big** surprise...

all the elves had wrapped their scarves round
right up to their eyes.

"We've had a horrid time!"
one little elf told Santa Claus.
"Ever since you went your wife has
air pooped without pause!"

"Ho, ho, ho!" said Santa.
"Sprouts are more fun than I knew!
I think I'll eat mine up next year
so I can join in too!"

So if you wake on Christmas night
and smell a certain **stink**,
just look up to the sky and give
old Santa Claus a wink!